Flow, Flow, Flow

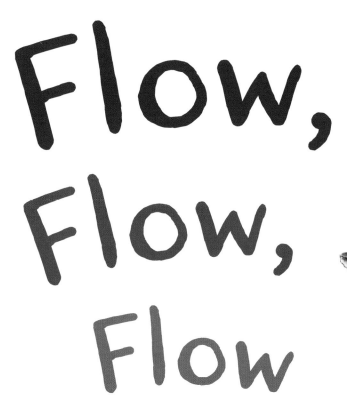

Flow, Flow, Flow

ANDRÉE SALOM

illustrated by IVETTE SALOM

Enjoy things with pleasure,
and delight in their flow.
Some things flow in,
some others go.

Enjoy the sun rising
until about noon.

Then enjoy the sun setting,
and say "Hi" to the moon.

In time every bubble goes
POP, **POP**, pop, **POP**.
Endings begin, and beginnings don't stop.

Enjoy tasty ice cream until it's all gone.
Munch away on the cone—then?

Have fun on the lawn!

Before new adventures, we get to let go
and say goodbye to a moment ago.

Share beautiful moments
with friends at the zoo,

then flow on forward.

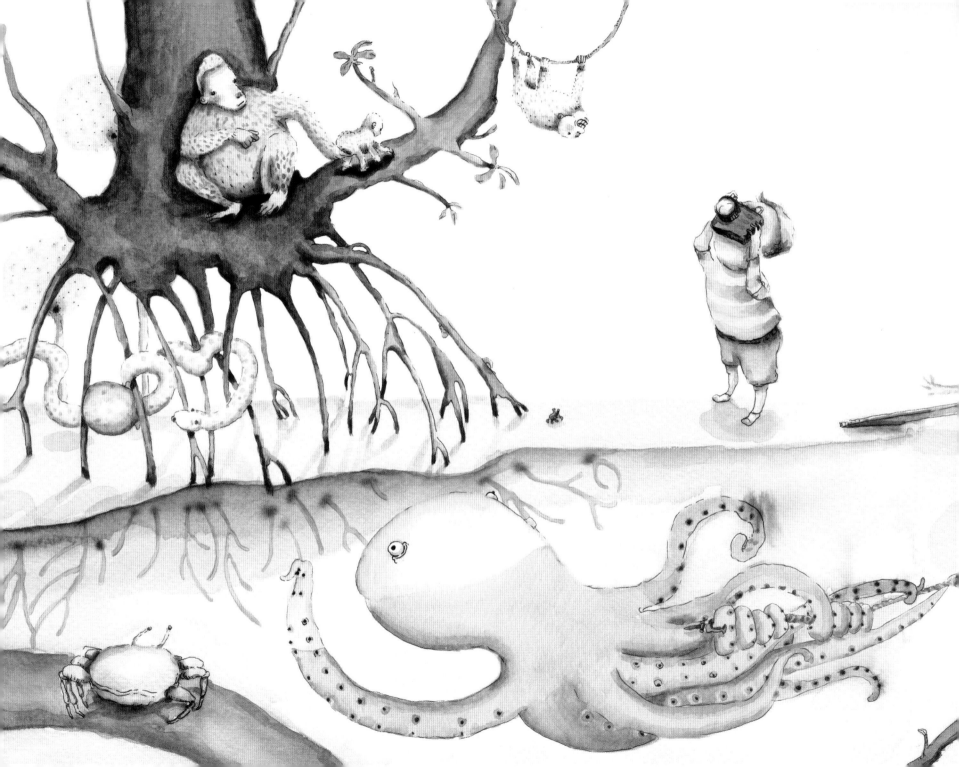

Notice the goodies
to which you hold on.
Are there any that you cling to,
even after they're gone?

Not every sweet
can always stay close.

Some of them go
when the wind of life blows.

Some of life's treats
are close-by and yummy.

But too much of those
can bring pain to your tummy.

Sometimes by using
big deep exhales,

we can better enjoy

life's small details.

Notice the choices that each moment brings.

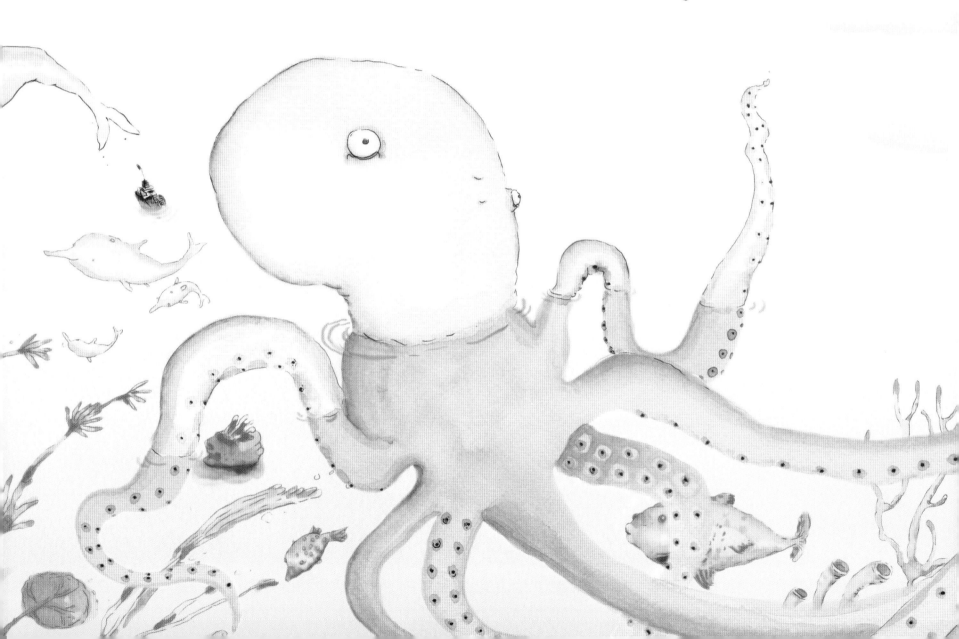

And notice the space
connecting all things.

When we're open to trust
we can soften our grip,

and then meet life's changes
with a slight smile or skip.

Enjoy things with pleasure, let everyone grow.

When it's time to move on, let life

flow, flow, flow, flow.

To our Mother and Father. Thank you for the many magical rides!

WISDOM PUBLICATIONS

199 Elm Street

Somerville, MA 02144 USA

wisdompubs.org

Library of Congress Cataloging-in-Publication Data

Names: Salom, Andrée, author. | Salom, Ivette, illustrator.

Title: Flow, flow, flow / by Andrée Salom; illustrated by Ivette Salom.

Description: Somerville, MA: Wisdom Publications, 2018. |

Identifiers: LCCN 2017023334 (print) | LCCN 2017040982 (ebook) | ISBN 9781614293415 (ebook)

ISBN 1614293414 (ebook) | ISBN 9781614293309 (hardcover: alk. paper)

Subjects: LCSH: Buddhism—Juvenile literature. | Buddhist stories.

Classification: LCC BQ4032 (ebook) | LCC BQ4032 .S24 2018 (print) | DDC 294.3/4432—dc23

LC record available at https://lccn.loc.gov/2017023334

ISBN 978-1-61429-330-9   ebook ISBN 978-1-61429-341-5

22 21 20 19 18   5 4 3 2 1

Cover and interior design by Annie Hirshman. Set in Gargle Regular.

Wisdom Publications' books are printed on acid-free paper and meet the guidelines for permanence
and durability of the Production Guidelines for Book Longevity of the Council on Library Resources.

Printed in the PRC.